Kiss & Tell Tail 3

~O~

Reverse Harem Fairy Tales

Book 3

TIMEA TOKES

Copyright © 2020 Timea Tokes

All rights reserved.

ISBN: 9798689817255

DEDICATION

To all my lovely readers out there. Remember, no matter what your dreams are (naughty or not), you have everything you need to make them come true.

If you love my writing style, please check out my other titles on Amazon, and follow me on my blog & website for a FREE pdf copy of Squirm Under My Watch, FREE Audiobooks, and other goodies, to say a personal thank you to you all.

I am also hosting a monthly signed paperback giveaway, with at least 2 winners each month. So, please stay tuned, and share the love that's deep inside all of you.

Thank you!

www.timeatokes.com

ACKNOWLEDGMENTS

All characters and events in these stories are purely fictional, therefore any resemblance to real people (living or dead) or events is a coincidence.

All characters would be at least 18 years of age, too, should they be real.

Caution: Contains descriptive sex scenes and adult contents.

Intended for a mature audience of at least 18+ (or more, depending on your country of residence and the local law).

Chapter 1

~o~

I glance behind me once more before crossing the threshold to her den, my heart filled with trepidation, my hands tingling. I had a feeling of being followed all the way down here, but then again, down here anything goes. I'm no longer in my father's kingdom, and neither am I protected. I know as well as Sebastian does that even if he did offer to come with me, I would still have to face the sea-witch on my own.

Partly because my mission is now between her and me, and partly because she has wanted to talk to me for a long time now. Of course, Sebastian doesn't know that bit, and I don't intend to tell him either once I get back. My mind wanders to all the possibilities and my feeling of dread is threatening to take over my sanity.

What if I never go back to him?

Not because I don't want to, but because she won't let me. But no, I can't think like that right now. I'm here to ask her a favour, and I know there will be a price to pay. Part of me wonders whether it's worth it, but the same part also knows that I don't have a choice.

I need to follow my true nature, and I can't deny Sebastian the pleasures this union will bring us. And, if I'm honest, I am a little bit in love with the idea of meeting Eric again. A smile creeps up my lips as I recall the time I first met him. Some would call it an accident, but I know it was destiny.

'Finally. I thought you would never make it.'

Ursula's thundering voice brings me back to reality, sending an unpleasant tingle down my spine. I inhale sharply, looking deep into her eyes. Unlike her sister, Medusa, Ursula expects you to make eye contact. That's her way of reading your soul. But to my surprise she shakes her head, beckoning me closer.

The water begins to whirl around me and I'm being pulled to her. My breath hitches when she places an icy finger under my chin, lifting it up. Her breath freezes mid-air as she whispers, her purple lips revealing razor-sharp teeth:

'I know why you are here. And I must say, I'm glad you made the right choice.'

My eyebrows shoot up and I mutter under my breath:

'You are? I did?'

Her laughter fills the cave with echoes, and my heart with fear. I swallow down bile, feeling sick all of a sudden. Isn't this supposed to be a good thing? My mother's warning rings in my mind: with Ursula, there is always a price to pay. My mother had to give up her singing voice for ever. I wonder what my price will be. As if sensing the way my thoughts are headed (and completely ignoring my questions), she swims up to the shelf behind her cauldron, reaching for a bottle of clear liquid.

'You know, my child, even the right choice leads us down the wrong path sometimes. And to avoid that, we will set up some ground rules.'

My heart skips a beat and I watch her back as she takes a few more bottles down from the shelf, moving onto the one next to it.

'There will be some trials you need to complete, and the change won't happen overnight. It won't be pleasant, either.'

I furrow my brows. Isn't she supposed to sell this whole magic stuff to me? She laughs again, turning towards me, juggling a bunch of vials.

'Come here, child.'

It's a gentle command, and yet I'm being pulled by that invisible force again, my tail moving on its own accord. Once flush up against her, she shoots me a brilliant smile, suddenly dropping the vials and grabbing my hands. I gasp as the iciness seeps into my skin, watching as the bottles float around us, swirling faster and faster.

'What's happening?'

I whimper, but she places an icy finger on my lips, silencing me.

'Do you want to see the future, or not?'

My eyes go wide and all I can do is nod. Her smile widens and she nods, placing her hand back on my own.

'Then close your eyes and calm your mind.'

As strange as it sounds, I comply and I'm suddenly back at my dad's palace. The difference is, however, that this time I'm there with Sebastian, Eric and another, blonde merman I don't recognise. They all have gorgeous tails of their own, and I blush at the way they all look at me. Something is off though, I can feel it. My head feels heavy, so I reach up, only to find a silver crown. I break contact and Ursula frowns at me. But I can't help it.

'What is going to happen to my father if I do this?'

I hiss, surprising both of us. Ursula purses her lips. I don't think she is used to mermaids raising their voices at her.

'You do realise that I could sniff you out with the snap of my fingers, yes?'

She purrs and I involuntarily start shaking. Despite my fear though, I find courage in the image she showed me. If she didn't need me, I would be dead already.

'You could, yes. But we both know you won't do that. You need me as much as I need you. The only question is what for?'

She regards me for a long moment, but I meet her eyes. I haven't come this far to back down now. I know I have a lot to be thankful for already, but I want to have it all. Ursula finally nods, throwing her hands up in the air in mock defeat. She isn't fooling me, the same way I'm not fooling her.

'Well, aren't you the clever one? To answer your question, your dad will be fine. You don't know this, but a mermaid princess can only become her true self when she marries her three merman. That's the same moment she gets the silver crown, an indication of her rank. And no, your dad will be fine for hundreds of years to come. Plenty of time for you to learn how to rule.'

Her words sooth me, but I'm not sure I can believe her. I clear my throat, remembering suddenly what she asked of my mother.

'Okay, fair enough. But what's in it for you?'

She shrugs, picking up a vial from mid-air and examines it, as if seeing it for the first time.

'I said you get three husbands. I didn't say you can choose them, did I?'

Seeing the horror and confusion on my face, sha waves her arms dismissively, returning her gaze to the vial. It's filled with a dark brown goo. For some reason, my eyes are fixed on it, too.

'Relax, you can keep your precious merman and your handsome prince. It's the third husband you don't get to choose.'

I gulp, contemplating my options. If the image was true, then this mystery merman will be devoted to me, and all I felt for him in the vision was pure love. Maybe with time I can accept that this choice is taken away from me. I'm about to say something when Ursula raises a finger, silencing me once again.

'There is more. Three more things, to be precise.'

I straighten my back.

'Three? My mother only had to give up one thing...'

Her evil eyes dart to mine and whatever I was going to say next gets lost in her gaze.

'She never told you, did she? Oh well, that's water under the bridge now. So, the three things...'

She gives me a moment to recover from what she just said, then continues:

'Number one: you spend a year as my slave, while also sleeping with the man I chose for you, here, in my world. You can't go back to your precious Sebastian, and you can't go back to your father, either. Don't worry, they will know you are safe. Any questions?'

I open my mouth, but before I could react, she adds:

'Good. Now, number two is a bit more complicated than the first one. You see, I work with true love, and I have my own rules. In a years' time, you will get to love my son, and once the one year is done and you served me well, you can go and collect your prize. But there's a catch.'

She gives me a bit more time this time, so I clear my throat, saying:

'I think I can survive one year here. I haven't seen your son yet, but if that's the price I need to pay, then so be it. Now, tell me what the catch is, because all you've given me is reason to doubt your intensions.'

She regards me coolly, eventually shrugging.

'My son isn't as bad as you think he is. He wields magic, but not the way I do. He likes to say that he chose the right side.'

She spits on the floor, as if his admission was something nasty. It makes me wonder why he can't choose his own bride, but it kind of makes sense. And I'm beginning to realise part of the catch, too. If I marry her son, our child will have a rightful claim to the throne one day. And that's something my father would never accept. Ursula clears her throat, looking straight into my eyes. Challenging me.

'The catch is that you have to find your own way to make Eric fall in love with you and kiss you with true love's first kiss. Those conditions are non-negotiable. Oh, and of course, you will have exactly three days to do so.'

Three days to make him fall in love with me? I saved his life once and we did meet a few times on the rocks, but nothing ever happened. Not really. So, I have to marry Ursula's son as well as the two men I have chosen to be my companions for life, and now she is telling me that if I don't execute the plan in three days, all will be lost. But what will be lost exactly? She still isn't telling me what will happen is I refuse, or if I fail my mission. Apart from ending up with a broken heart, of course. My eyebrows furrow when I realise another loophole in her story.

'And what about the third thing?'

She raises an eyebrow in response.

'Pardon?'

I nod, swimming around in tiny circles.

'You said there was a third part to the deal. You only told me two.'

Her laughter sends icy shards of fear down my spine once again.

'Oh, that? Well, it's nothing, really.'

I let out a shaky breath, looking her deep in the eyes again, preparing myself for the part of the deal when I have to give up everything. Her eyes reflect authority and a sense that she already won, and mine reflect determination.

'Knowing you, it's everything. And I won't sign the contract until I know.'

She looks at me for what feels like for ever before nodding. She reaches an icy finger out, then thinking better of it, she moves it to scratch the corner of her mouth. An involuntary shudder runs through me anyway. I might have said that I would survive a year as her slave, but I have no idea about the kind of stuff she could do to me.

'Very well. My third condition is the thing you will need to give up. Your memory. You won't have any recollection of any of this, well, after the year is over, that is. From the moment you step foot on shore, you won't know who you are, where you are from, or who Eric is.'

Panic rises within me, but she continues:

'You won't remember me or your precious mermaid. None of it, not even your father. But you will have all your charms at hand, and you will have two beautiful legs. Besides, if you play your cards right, you will end up getting your memories back. Just not until the deed is done.'

She leaves me alone for a while, to help me cope with the new information. I am so heartbroken that I even forget to ask what happens if I don't succeed. In a way, it doesn't matter. With a sinking heart, I sign on the dotted line, sealing my fate.

~o~

Chapter 2

~o~

It's been two months since I signed that dreadful contract, and yet I'm still waiting for it to bit me in the ass. A sad smile appears on my lips when I realise that I just uttered another famous saying I learnt from the humans. I close my eyes, picturing Sebastian next to me, laughing, telling me how silly I am for using all these weird phrases.

I haven't seen him since that day when I first swam into Ursula's lair, and I assume it's her magic that keeps me sane right now. All I feel is a dull ache in my chest, but even that's overshadowed by my excitement at the new adventure I'm going to embark on. Soon. I've been counting the days since I arrived.

I think the fact that I will be able to give Sebastian what he needs when this is over, and we will be reunited helps cope with the pain of being separated from him. And Ursula kept her promise. She put a spell on everyone, making sure they knew I was safe, but didn't ask many questions as to where I was. They are at peace with my disappearance, and although that hurts a little, I understand that it's for their benefit as much as for mine.

On worse days I question my reasons for doing this and whether it's really worth it, but anytime I try to raise my concerns, Ursula just shrugs, telling me that I made a choice. I can still take it back, but I can't go back to the way things were. And she is right, I can feel it in my gut. If I gave up before even trying, I wouldn't be able to face Sebastian, because I would know that I'm consciously depriving him of his own happiness.

And, to be fair to Ursula, she hasn't been horrible to me. Actually, she has been surprisingly sweet, asking me every day how I felt. And, depending on my reply, she would mutter something under her breath, giving me easier or harder tasks. Some days all I have to do is feed her eels, then I'm free to wander around.

'Everything alright, my dear?'

Her raspy voice brings me back to reality and I fake a smile, raising the glass to my lips. The delicious burn of the red liquid makes me feel lightheaded.

'Indeed. I was just thinking about our arrangement. What is this, by the way?'

I ask, pointing at the red liquid, genuinely curious. She smiles at me, raising her own glass to her purple lips.

'It's a special type of alcohol humans drink all the time. To them it's quite mundane, really, but to us, it has a special effect.'

She looks away for a second and I hold my breath. As nice as she is to me now, I can't help but remember the stories my mum told me about her. Not to mention that I practically signed my soul over to her. When she looks at me again, her eyes are glazed over with emotion.

'I first tasted it with Finn's father, bless his soul. But anyway, since you have served me well for so long, I have a surprise for you. Close your eyes.'

I raise an eyebrow at her when she mention's her son or his father. Apart from the first night when I signed the contract, she never mentioned either of them. I didn't even know her son's name until now, let alone how he looks like. And then my other eyebrow shoots up when she asks me to close my eyes. Her laughter sends vibrations throughout the hall.

'You don't trust me, do you?'

I open my mouth to reply, but she shakes her head.

'No, don't answer that. Fine, keep your eyes open, but don't peek, okay?'

I nod, unable to speak. Something tells me that the surprise she has for me is her son. I know it sounds weird, but I have been sensing a strangely powerful presence here for the last couple of days, and I had a feeling that someone was watching me while I worked. My suspicions are confirmed when Ursula whisper-shouts through a door behind my back:

'You can come in now.'

Goosebumps rise on my skin as I listen to the door opening and closing, and every fibre in my body is telling me to run. But for some reason, I stay still, staring straight ahead. My head is heavy with the alcoholic beverage I drank, and my heart is fluttery with all the excitement and fear of this meeting. After all, the man I'm about to meet will be my husband, and I've been dreading this moment for the past two months. What if I can't grow to love him? What if Sebastian or Eric won't accept him?

'It's nice to meet you, Ariel.'

An unfamiliar, yet pleasant and calming voice says and I nod in response, as if lead by my instincts alone. My mind is clearly not functioning right now.

'The pleasure is all mine, Finn.'

He swims up in front of me and I gasp when I see him. He smiles, tiny dimples playing at either side of his lips. He reaches out a hand and I automatically take it, still in shock.

'Good. Now that the two of you met each other, it's time to organise the wedding.'

I must pale because Finn rolls his eyes at his mother, while placing a protective hand at the small of my back.

'Mum, stop it. You can't expect her to jump into my arms straight away. As I know you, you probably haven't even told her anything about me.'

I am unable to look at either one of them, and the strange fluttering in my heart grows stronger with every gentle movement of Finn's fingers on my back. I feel like I'm betraying Sebastian by feeling this way. I don't even know this guy. And yet, his scent is so familiar, and so is his touch. It's as if he touched me this way before, I just don't remember.

Ursula shrugs, looking away. She starts fiddling with her potions again, and it's my turn to roll my eyes, knowing too well that I will have to spend tomorrow rearranging those shelves.

'You are right, of course. Go and get to know each other properly and don't mind my silliness.'

Finn frowns and I blush, knowing too well from Ursula's tone what she is referring to. Is this how it is? I'm supposed to sleep with her son the moment I meet him? I am afraid to glance up at Finn, but I can't help it, my eyes move on their own accord. My breath hitches when I realise that he is looking straight back at me, his expression unreadable.

Time slows down and all I can see for a moment are his grey irises with a speckle of violet in them, boring into mine. It's as if I'm being sucked up into one of those whirlpools that I used to admire. When I can finally break the eye-contact, I glance down at his violet-black tentacles, wondering if they turn into legs the same way my tail does. Simply thinking about it is sending a tingle down my spine, and I can't allow him to notice how turned on I am.

I feel ashamed by the way I feel, if I'm honest. I thought all I ever wanted was Sebastian, and I truly believed that until I met Eric on that fateful day when his ship sank to the bottom of the ocean. Although he wasn't any more gorgeous that my merman, there was something so authoritative, so alluring in him that I couldn't resist.

At first I thought it was just a wayward desire, one that didn't need to be fulfilled. But then my mother told me about all the ways she desired her lovers, and how she had to choose. And now that I have met Finn, I already know that he will be my third choice. Contract or no contract, I would want him anyway, and I don't even know him yet.

Yes, I know, mermaids can be shallow sometimes, but I just can't help it. It's as if he was already part of my soul and my destiny. Ursula clears her throat and I blush some more, realising suddenly that I'm stroking one of Finn's tentacles. I glance up into a gorgeous smiling face.

'Let's go and get some air.'

My heart skips a beat, but I nod anyway. Finn takes my hand and we swim out of Ursula's lair and into the open ocean. I haven't left her place since I arrived, and I'm surprised by how much Finn trusts me to be out here. But then again, I wouldn't run, and he knows that.

'Sorry if that was awkward. It isn't like I ever brought any of my girlfriends home before.'

Finn's attempt at a joke doesn't go completely over my head and I smile at him, while also admiring all the wonders around us. My heart clenches at the thought that my happiness will be temporary. Finn must sense the way my thoughts are going, because he gives my hand a tight squeeze.

'Look, mum means well. I'm pretty sure she will tell you about the prophecy when you are ready, and then we can see how to proceed.'

I raise an eyebrow at him, studying his handsome features. For a moment, his features flicker and he looks different. His hair is longer, and he has a braided beard. His tentacles are also replaced by a black tail. But as soon as the image appears, it vanishes just as quickly and my focus returns to what Finn just said.

'A prophecy?'

He lets out a sigh, looking away.

'I want to tell you, but it isn't the right time yet. But yes, there is an ancient prophecy about the future of our race, and that's the main reason my mother made you sign that contract.'

He then turns to me, cupping my face gently. A shiver runs down my back, tingling my tail. I can feel the vibrations slowly turn me, and I bite my lower lip in anticipation.

'The prophecy isn't the only reason why I want to be with you though.'

He leans closer, his lips inches away from mine. Part of me wants to remind him that we hardly belong to the same race, considering that he is a sea witch and I'm a mermaid, but I let it go for now.

'Why do you want to be with me then?'

He places a featherlight kiss onto my nose, taking me by surprise, then grabs my hand again, pulling me closer to the surface. He doesn't look at me as he replies.

'Because we belong together.'

I expected him to tell me I was beautiful, clever, a princess, or something similar, but this? He must sense my confusion, because he adds quietly:

'We were together in our previous lives. All four of us.'

He trails off and my heart skips a beat. My mother told me about stories where mermaids got a second, or even a third chance at life. It normally happened if they failed to accomplish what they were supposed to do, then got reincarnated back into the ocean to start over again. Some retained their memories, some didn't, and if they failed again, they were thrown back into that whirlpool.

'Were we happy?'

I ask, trying to picture the four of us centuries ago. For some reason, doubting Finn doesn't even cross my mind. His eyes meet mine, and there is so much sadness in them that it breaks my heart to watch. I want to pull him in for a hug to comfort him, but I also realise how awkward that would be.

'Yes, very.'

I want to ask him what happened then, but he continues without me having to say anything:

'But we didn't fulfil the prophecy, so we are back again.'

He looks at me, eyes burning with unknown flames. I gulp back tears at a memory that lingers at the back of my mind.

'Why don't I remember if you do?'

I ask and he looks away. We reach the surface and I realise that he brought me to a very specific location. I take a deep breath, and instead of having a go at him, I ask calmly:

'Finn?'

He lets out another sigh, pulling me up onto a rock that's protruding out of the water. I breath in the salty air, watching my tail turn into a set of legs. I am too scared to glance Finn's way. I think I will have to prompt him to talk again, but he surprises me by saying:

'You don't remember because you asked my mother to take your memories away.'

I gasp, this time looking him straight in the eyes.

'Why on earth would I do that for?'

A sad smile appears on his lips as I dangle my feet off the rock. I barely notice that he is doing the same.

'Because something terrible happened that you wanted to forget. We all wanted to forget it, and the rest of us did.'

I raise an eyebrow, my heart going out to him.

'Except you?'

He nods, looking at the ship that's sailing in the distance. My heart is doing all sorts of crazy flips right now. Part of me wants to know what was so horrible that I wanted my memories gone, but another part of me knows that it doesn't matter. The rest of my memories will be gone soon as well anyway.

'You can pull this off, you know.'

Finn's voice is reaching me through a haze, and I watch with trepidation to see whether the ship is that ominous ship.

'What do you mean?'

It passes us and I release a breath I have been holding for too long. Eric must be safe and on shore, otherwise Ursula's contract would be worth nothing.

'All I'm saying that you did it before. I mean, you found us without remembering us, and you can do it again. And besides, I will be there to help you.'

I want to ask him how, but he suddenly leans in for a kiss, taking me by surprise. I automatically close my eyes, images of a past long gone flashing behind my closed eyelids, accompanied by a myriad of stars.

~o~

Chapter 3

~o~

After a moment Finn pulls away, breathing heavily. Seeing my confused expression he shrugs, smiling coyly.

'I'm sorry, I just couldn't help it. I used to worship you, you know…'

To give meaning to his words, he runs a hand up my naked thigh, making me shudder. I was careful not to look at his impressive body before, but now I glance over without shame. Sebastian said I needed to do this, and according to Ursula, I have to practice before the big deal. My heart is filled with mixed flutters of excitement and fear, sending tremors down my entire being. Us mermaids are blessed, really, but so are sea witches by the looks of it.

Finn's blackish-purple tentacles have been replaced by two muscular legs the moment we sat on the rock. His caressing hand reaches higher up and I let out a soft moan, tilting my head up towards the stars. Finn's words reach my subconscious as his hands reach the ball of my foot, rubbing the tender flesh gently. I relax into his touch. It might be his stories of us being together in a previous life, or the mention of the prophecy, but I feel like I no longer have a choice in this. I am lost in him the same way I'm lost in Sebastian and Eric.

'I used to kiss you in places nobody has kissed you before. Did you know, that here, for example…'

I glance down in time to watch him place a soft kiss underneath my toe. His grey eyes shine with a violet sheen, and I'm pretty sure he is using his magic on me, because spark after spark appears on my skin, travelling up to my pussy. I gasp when the first electric shock rocks my core.

'Is one of your erogenous zones, as the humans call it.'

I don't need to ask him what he means as my back automatically arches at his delicate touch.

'You used to do this to me and I didn't want to remember you? I'm such a monster.'

The half-joke doesn't go as planned. Finn stops massaging and kissing my foot, looking up at me with so much pain in his grey eyes that I regret what I said instantly.

'You aren't a monster, it's just... Ariel, please don't ask about that part of our past. I'm not ready to tell you yet.'

If I thought the hurt in his eyes was bad enough, I never knew what I was talking about. Hearing his strained voice makes my heart ache for him. Before I know what's happening, I have slipped down into the water, moving so that I'm right in front of him. Finn looks down at me incredulously and I rest my arms on his knees, fully aware of what's at my eye-level. But instead of looking at his cock, I decide to gaze deep into his eyes. I can only hope that my eyes don't betray me.

'Look, Finn, I know it's too early, and you probably think I'm crazy, but I want to help you. I really do.'

Without giving him a moment to think about this, I reach out to caress his cock. Unfortunately for me, he is too fast, grabbing my hand mid-air. I raise an eyebrow, but he shakes his head.

'No, my princess. I need to worship you, not the other way round.'

His words bring a pang of sadness, because they remind me of the time when Sebastian did almost the same. I nod anyway, trying not to let my frustration show. Apparently, I can't act as well as I thought I could.

'Ariel, please. Let me do this for you. Sebastian wouldn't want you to miss out on pleasure just because he isn't around. Isn't this what the whole quest is about?'

Finn is right, although it makes me wonder what Sebastian is up to nowadays. Ursula only promised me that he will know I'm safe, and that he won't be looking for me. But she never cared to reveal the reasons why. Finn shocks me once again by nodding, as if listening into my inner conversation with myself.

'Can you read my mind?'

I ask incredulously and he looks away, his grip on my hand easing up a bit.

'Yes. I can also send you telepathic messages.'

He suddenly turns his attention back towards me, bringing my hands up to his lips.

'When you are up there without your memories, I can't tell you exactly what happened. But I will send you clues and warnings. I will be watching you closely and make sure you get Eric to fall in love with you.'

He says this with so much eagerness that I raise an eyebrow.

'You would do that for me?'

He nods, releasing my hands.

'Yes. All three of us would do anything for you. And that's why you need to do this for us.'

Now it's my turn to nod. Although I can't probe him for more answers about the prophecy or why I gave up my memories willingly the first time, I have all the answers I need for now. I trust Finn, and if Ursula was right and he does use his magic for good, then I don't have anything to worry about.

'Fine, I will do everything I can to make this happen for us. All of us.'

A timid smile plays at Finn's gorgeous lips as he places another kiss onto my palm. I smile back at him, although with a bit more cheekiness. As far as I'm concerned, the time for talking is over. And if he is willing to risk everything for me, even getting discovered by his mother, then I need to be willing to do everything for him, too.

'I will be back in a minute.'

I whisper, my eyes begging him to trust me. He watches me for a moment, but nods eventually, curiosity taking over. I chuckle before going for a mission of my own. My legs give way to my tail once again and I swim in my ocean one last time. Except this time I don't feel like I'm running out of time, or that my choice is difficult to make. I know I can have it all, and I'm about to start.

Once I find what I'm looking for, I make my way back towards the surface. Finn visibly relaxes. Did he think I swam away, never to return? I shoot him a radiant smile before taking up my previous position between his legs. His toes are soaking in the ocean, but his erection is still there. The idea that I have this effect on him (on three men, actually) fills me with a weird sense of pride.

'What are you up to?'

He asks suspiciously, but I place a finger on his lips.

'Quiet now. Remember, we are out in the open. You don't want to attract the bad type of crowd.'

He opens his lips again, probably wanting to argue that indeed he is the head of that crowd and he doesn't have to be afraid of them, but one look from me silences him for good. I nod to myself, producing the seaweed.

'Besides, you only know the type of sex we had when it was the four of us in a different lifetime. I'm different now. I've learnt a lot from the humans. So, for a change, let me worship you.'

I watch his Adam's apple bob up and down as he swallows hard.

'I don't think this is a good idea...'

I shake my head, then swim around the rock, moving behind him. I can practically hear his heartbeat quicken, making me wonder whether I can somehow share his magic. Before I could speculate any longer, his voice steers me in the right direction:

'Whenever we are near, we all share our magic. But you have your own magic, too.'

I shrug. I have never been the kind of girl who would care about such things. Instead I change the topic as smoothly as I can, tying one piece of the seaweed around his hands in the meantime, forcing them to stay behind his back for now.

'I see. Well, I'm sorry that these will have to do as props. I don't exactly have time to get to my secret cave.'

I swim back in front of Finn, and his eyes are filled with a violet heat now as he cocks his head to the side.

'Your secret sex cave, you mean?'

I blush, biting my lower lip. His eyes follow the movement, and my eyes go wide. I reach up and place the other piece of seaweed around his head, covering his eyes. Once I'm done, I whisper into his ear:

'That's exactly what I mean. I might take you there one day. But for now, my plans are right here and right now.'

And with that, I sink between his thighs and he lets out a groan of anticipation. I reach for his cock, licking my lips, finally letting this new side of me come to the surface.

~o~

Chapter 4

~o~

Part of me knows that I should have waited a little longer. The same part of me feels ashamed of what I'm doing right now. But there is another part of me that's enjoying every minute of this. Finn's loud moan reminds me that I probably should have put something in his mouth, and not just on his eyes, but it's too late now.

I trace the tip of his cock with my little finger, scraping the underside with my nail. This is something Sebastian taught me. He said it would drive any man crazy with desire. Now that I think about it, he must have known even back then that I will need to apply this knowledge on someone else.

'Please, Ariel, don't torture me anymore. I can't take it much longer...'

My nail accidentally scrapes across the tip of his cock, and his whole shaft jumps under my hand.

'Yes, you can. Don't you have magic? Use it to help you.'

His cock jerks again, and I can't wait any longer myself. Sending up a silent prayer, hoping that Sebastian will forgive me and understand, I place my lips at the tip of Finn's pulsating cock. He whimpers when I part my lips, barely enough to take his whole girth in, but enough to tease him some more. I make out that he is too big for me (which isn't entirely a lie), taking several attempts to take him between my lips.

'That's not how my magic works...'

He says between gritted teeth, and I almost feel sorry for him, but I'm pretty sure he did stuff like this to me all the time. Lead by a sudden idea I pop my head back up, and he releases a shaky breath.

'Could I do it?'

Even with the seaweed-blindfold on, Finn looks confused, so I decide to elaborate:

'I mean, could I keep your erection up with my own magic? You did say I had my own…'

I trail off, my fingers running up and down his shaft. A seagull lands next to us, plucking at a loose feather. A wicked smile creeps up my lips as I watch the bird, snatching the dispatched feather before it could be carried away by either the winds or the waves.

'I'm not telling you anymore. Now please, do something.'

I raise an eyebrow, and even though he can't see me, I roll my eyes at him.

'Oh, so now you want me to do something? You wanted me to stop a moment ago.'

I'm pretty sure he rolls his eyes at me this time.

'You know what I meant. Please make me cum so I can worship you as well.'

The idea sends a jolt of electricity down my spine and I decide not to waste any more time on talking. Brushing my hair aside, I bob down onto his shaft. This time it disappears into my mouth without any effort from my part, taking him by surprise.

It isn't until I tickle his balls with the feather though that he jumps, almost making me choke on his cock.

'Fuck! That's so intense. What are you doing?'

Oh, that?

I let go of his cock with an unladylike slurping sound, wiping my mouth with the back of my hand.

'Oh, that? It's a feather. Humans use it to cause immense pleasure.'

He coughs and for a moment he has me worried. Right up to the moment when he jumps off the rock and pulls his blindfold off.

'I know what a feather is for, thank you very much.'

He says darkly and it's my turn to gulp. I try to swim away from him, but he grabs me by the waist, lifting me up onto the rock. I whimper when he picks up the seaweed, tying my hands together behind my back, the same way I did to him earlier.

'I'm not sure I like this turn of events.'

I say, but Finn just shrugs, chuckling.

'I couldn't exactly wait for you, could I? You were too busy playing. But now it's my turn.'

I gasp as the feather connects with my sensitive skin. Finn doesn't even bother covering my eyes. He knows he doesn't have to. I lean back, resting on the rock while he pushes my knees apart, and opens my pussy lips with his fingers.

'You are so goddamn beautiful. And I have been waiting for this for so long...'

My breath hitches as I'm waiting for his lips to connect with my clit, but it's his hand that connects with it instead. Hard.

'Ouch, what was that for?'

I ask incredulously, but his answer gets lost between my folds. I cry out in a mixture of pain and pleasure when his tongue presses down on my clit and he tickles my asshole with the feather. Somehow when he slapped my pussy, he made it so extremely sensitive that I can't even last a minute without coming all over his mouth.

I am panting heavily, trying to wriggle free, but he holds me firmly in place. I look up at the stars, counting my own ones that are dancing behind my eyelids. When Finn pushes two fingers inside my folds and moves the feather to tease my left nipple, another wave of orgasm rocks my body. I forget what I asked him, but he clearly remembers, because he chooses this moment to come up for air, his fingers still pumping in and out of my pussy.

'That was for you tying me up and not letting me worship you.'

I want to object, but he suddenly pulls his fingers out, slapping my clit hard once again, sending me on a never-ending ride of exploding stars and waterworks. My pussy is drenched, and I find it difficult to breathe, even though I never have any difficulties of the sort. Not on earth, not in water.

'And that?'

I ask in a feeble voice, but he simply smirks at me, licking his way up my slit. I wish I had something to hold onto, but I don't. He doesn't let me pull my legs close, either, so I'm forced to ride the orgasm out as it is: rough, demanding and shattering.

'That was for asking too many questions.'

I roll my eyes at him before he licks me to oblivion. My head is spinning, and it takes me a moment to realise that I'm actually spinning out of control.

'Finn, what's happening?'

I ask in utter horror, but he just shrugs, slowly fading out of view. His words echo in my mind; a reassurance that everything will be okay. But I don't believe him this time. I'm being sucked in by a whirlpool, and everything I know is fading away. I want to shout and scream, telling Ursula that she is breaking our contract, that I'm not ready yet. I thought I had more time.

But it's no use. I can't speak, and even her name doesn't bode well on my tongue. I'm losing track of time, and all there is at the back of my mind is complete darkness. And then I start falling...

~o~

A tempting taste of other, bite-size erotica, from the naughty pen of Timea Tokes:

~o~

A SPECIAL CUP OF COFFEE
(SAMPLE)

Don't worry, this is a first for me, too..."
Ah, is that supposed to comfort me?
Very promising.

I try to pull on the restraints, but he has tied me up tightly. My heart is pounding, and I can't see a thing because of the blindfold. All I can do is wait helplessly until he figures out his next move, wondering how could I have gotten myself into this mess.

A mere hour ago I was sitting at the bar, minding my own business, drinking heavily, as if there was no tomorrow. Right up to the moment when the bartender offered to make me a special cup of coffee. Which I'm still waiting for, by the way.

Just saying.

Okay, I wasn't that naïve to think that we would actually be drinking coffee, cuddling on his couch, no. And as I said, I didn't want that anyway. I wanted hot, steamy, and kinky sex. And although he hasn't touched me yet, not in that way anyway, this whole situation is kinky alright.

"Just try to relax and clear your mind..."

He is really getting into this. Does he have a guidebook that he is citing from? I must admit that hearing his voice alone makes me shiver all over. It is sexy as hell, and I can already feel the previous dampness of my thong worsening by the minute. I wonder how long is he going to keep me suspended like this? It's funny how you lose all of your senses when you can't see.

No kidding!

Although I can hear his voice, but only when he allows me to, and I still can't tell where it's coming from. For all I know he could be standing in the doorway, ready to lock me in, leaving me to suffer for God knows how long. I sure as hell hope he isn't planning to make that special cup of coffee r*ight now.*

But judging by what he just said, I guess I need to do the opposite. In fact, my mind is the only thing that's working perfectly well right now. And my survival instincts, of course. I begin to regret that I didn't listen to my friends. I should have waited for this kind of kink until I knew the guy, let alone trusted him.

Oh my God, I don't even know his name!

"You might feel a little bit cold. Try not to wiggle too much, okay?"

Okay, I was wrong. All my nerves are on edge, and I want to scream from the ice-cold sensation that's burning my left nipple right now.

Little bit cold?

Whatever he put on me makes me want to swear and scream, except I can't. All I can give out is a tiny whimper through my gritted teeth. I want to tell him to stop, to let me go, feeling embarrassed and exposed all of a sudden.

But as quickly as the thought forms in the back of my mind, it evaporates just as quickly when he takes my erect nipple into his mouth. His hot, wet tongue is a relief from the ice-cold sensation, and yet it feels a tad bit more painful, maybe because I am more sensitive than I ever was. He bites down gently, and I can feel the coldness on my right nipple, while he is stroking my left one with his tongue.

I gasp, getting lost in the mixed sensations of hot and cold, pain and pleasure. But it doesn't last long, and as much as I wanted him to stop at first, now I wish that he would continue the sweet torture. An involuntary moan leaves my lips, and he lets out a small chuckle.

"Don't worry, I have only just started."

His words send a jolt of electricity right down to my lady parts, and I'm sure I blush a little, too. I think about my black strapless dress, the black lace push-up bra and the black high heels scattered around the room. I'm not even sure he is wearing anything right now, as after a few passionate kisses, he moved straight onto the subject. He promised it to be fun, erotic and orgasmic.

The last part convinced me, and I'm more and more sure that he is a man who keeps his promises...

~o~

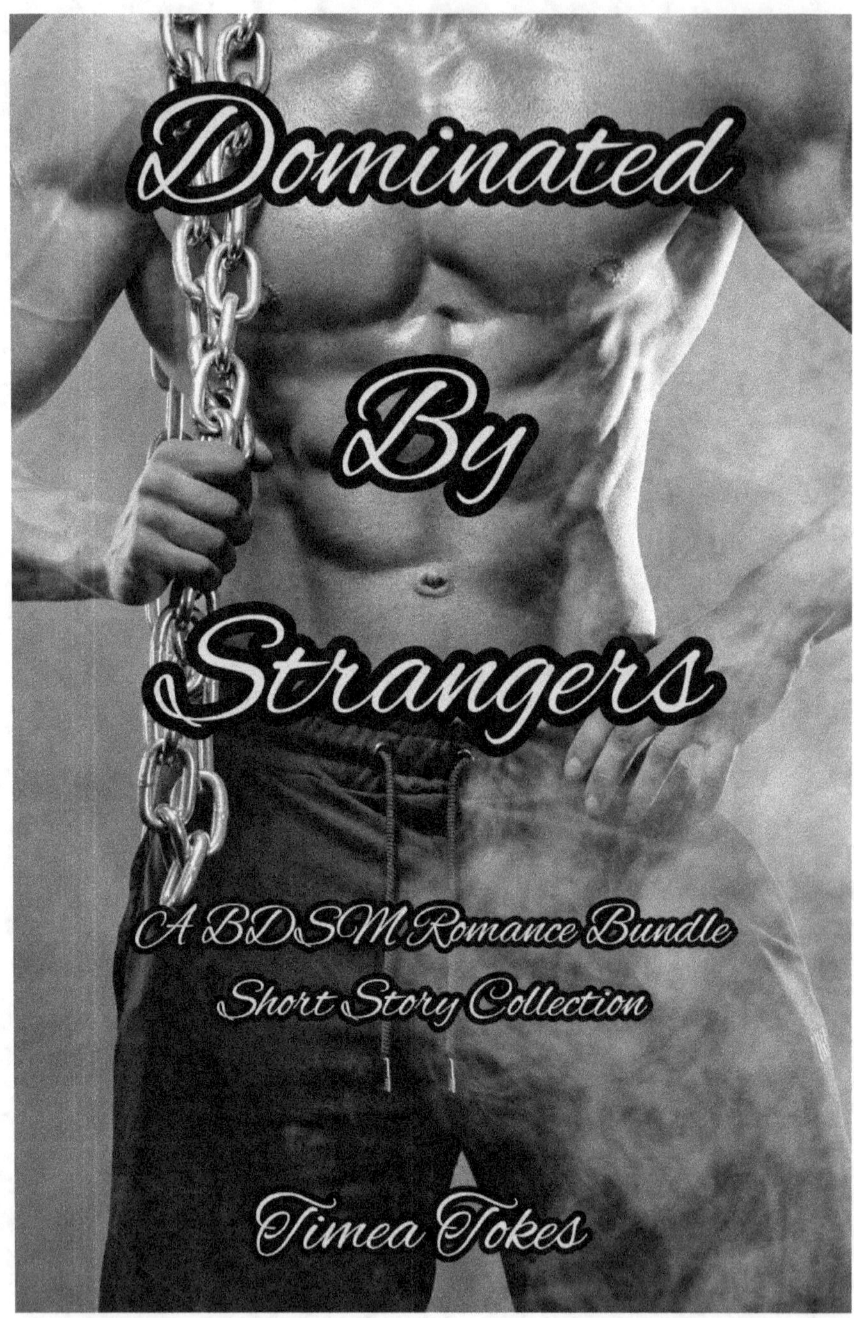

Dominated
By
Strangers
A BDSM Romance Bundle
Short Story Collection
Timea Tokes

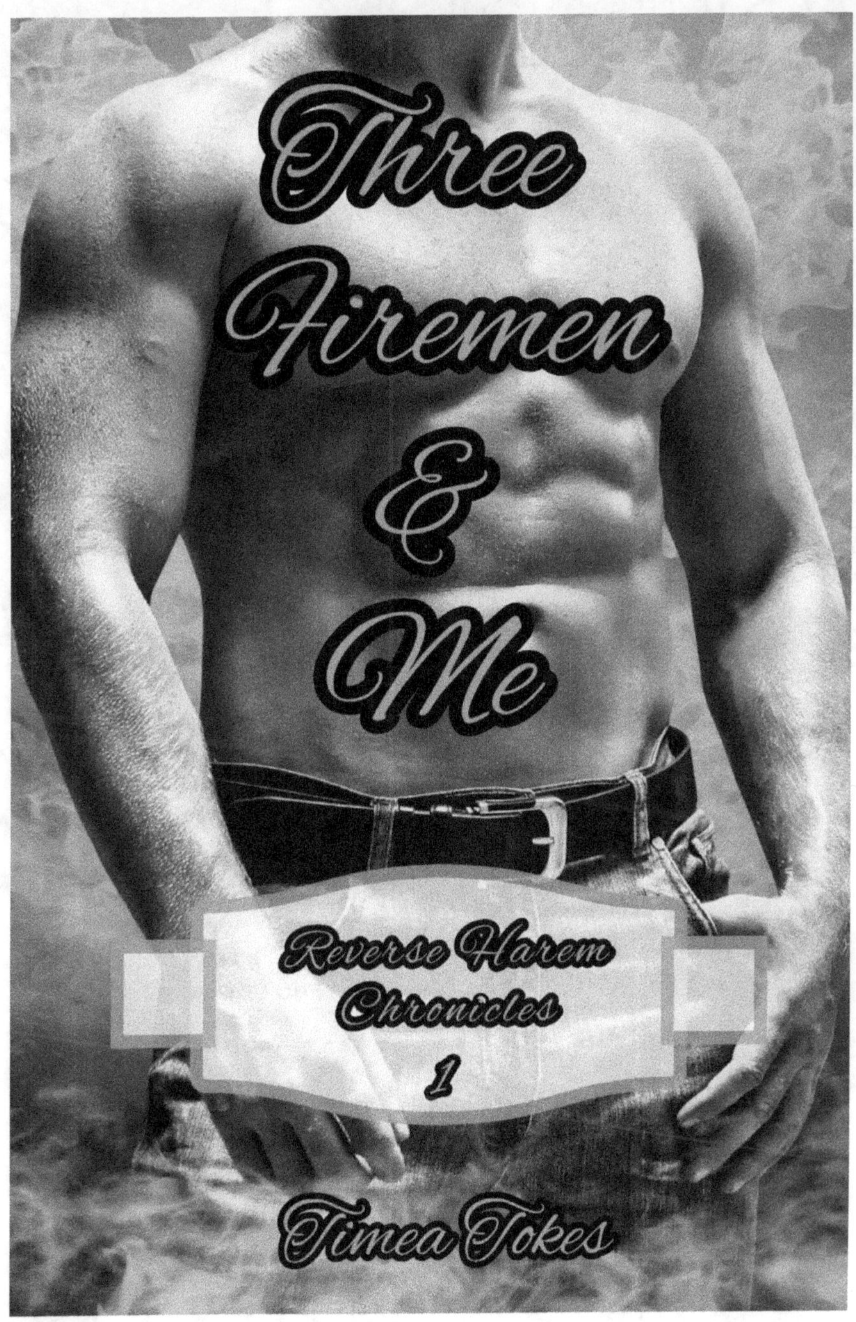

Three
Firemen
&
Me
Reverse Harem
Chronicles
1
Timea Tokes

<u>**Other Books by Timea Tokes:**</u>

<u>**Paranormal Romance:**</u>
Her First Secret
Her Secret Admirer
His Secret Love
Their Last Secret
Her First And Last Secret Admirer

<u>**Erotic Short Stories:**</u>

<u>**Reverse Harem Chronicles:**</u>
Three Firemen & Me
Three Firemen & Me 2
Three Policemen & Me
Three Policemen & Me 2
Three Billionaires & Me
Three Billionaires & Me 2

<u>**Reverse Harem Fairy Tales:**</u>
Kiss & Tell Tail
Kiss & Tell Tail 2

<u>**BDSM:**</u>
A Special Cup of Coffee – Pain and Pleasure

<u>**Hotwife:**</u>
Stuck & Shared

<u>**Holiday Erotica:**</u>
Mistletoe Boss
Dating The Author (Why Choose)
My Hitch-Hiking Valentine
The Bucket List
The Bucket List 2 - Damsel in Distress
Truth or Dare?

Exhibitionist & Voyeur:
Squirm Under My Watch
How About the Rooftop?
Don't Make A Sound

Paranormal Erotica:
Conjured Lover

The Plumber Series:
Seducing the Plumber 1: Sweet Time Waiting
Seducing the Plumber 2: Sweet Torture

The Escort Series:
The Escort's Taxi Ride
The Escort's Taxi Ride 2
The Escort's Taxi Ride 3

The Good Neighbor Series (Bisexual, Why Choose):
The Good Neighbor – An Unexpected Threesome
The Good Neighbor – Tied up by the Knight
The Good Neighbor – In the Backseat
The Good Neighbor – The Massage
The Good Neighbor – Guilty Pleasures

Sweet yet Naughty:
Forgotten
Blue Highlights

Gay:
The Stranger

Collections of Short Stories:
You Had Me At Kinky
You Had Me At Steamy
You Had Me At Rough

<u>Coming Soon:</u>

The Plumber's Excuse (2020)
Three Billionaires & Me 3 (2020)
Kiss & Tell Tail 4 (2020)
A Cupid Mistake (2021)
Hell's Bride (2021)

<u>Follow Timea Tokes on:</u>

Amazon @timea_tokes

Twitter @timea_tokes

Facebook @herfirstsecret

Goodreads @timea_tokes

<u>Sign up to her newsletter, and have a look at her blog for more bite-size erotica, paranormal romance, reviews and more:</u>

www.timeatokes.com

<u>Note from the Author, Timea Tokes:</u>

~o~

My dear, lovely Reader, thank you for taking the time to read my story! I really hope you enjoyed it as much as I did writing it. As always, your feedback is highly valued and much appreciated.

Please do take the time to scroll to the end of the book and leave a review. It would mean the World to me!

And remember, this story is all about your pleasure.

On the next page, you can learn a bit more about me and why I write, but you will also find author interviews (and much more) on my website.

~o~

ABOUT THE AUTHOR

~o~

I have been writing short stories and poems since a young age, but my ultimate goal was creating a novel. Or a series, rather. Now, with my four paranormal romance novels published, as well as more than 30 erotica titles under my belt, , I think I can say that it came true - but this only fuels my desire to write more. After all, we are allowed to dream the same dream (over and over again) - and that's exactly what I'm planning to do :)

I enjoy helping people in any way possible, and I really hope that my books will prove to be inspirational in a way. Whether readers are looking for a swift (and steamy) erotic story, or a paranormal romance, I want them to associate themselves with my characters and realize stuff about themselves in the process.

Yes, even the bad things. Because, in life, there is no black and white, only colors. Therefore, I don't think any of my characters are either good or bad, but rather a little bit of both.

Aren't we all?

Well, if you never had guilty thoughts, never had any self-confidence issues, or if you never wanted something (or someone) who belonged to someone else, then probably my books won't be for you. But, who knows, I might be able to show you a different perspective. I like to experiment with different genres, and new concepts and ideas.

I really enjoy learning as much as I can about people, what makes them tick (and live, laugh, cry, and sigh). In fact, I think our World (and those beyond) are so diverse, ten thousand lifetimes wouldn't be enough to explore it all. But one thing I truly believe in: those who belong in your life will find a way there. Therefore my stories are usually based on chance encounters and ordinary events that take an unexpected turn.

Like a blind date on Valentine's day, or a haircut, or a new job. Who says you can't meet someone 'accidentally'; while going to the hairdresser, someone you lost contact with 500 years ago? Trust me, you can. You just need to brace every day (and every book) with open eyes - and an open heart.

Just remember: my stories are all about you, and you alone. If they capture your attention (and your heart), then I've done my 'job'. I regularly try to release new content, both on Amazon and my blog. Please feel free to have a look, and sign up to my newsletter.

And, just so you know: I care about your opinion, very much so. Whether you liked my work or you didn't, I would be honored if you let me know what it meant for you. It would mean the world to me!

~o~

1. When did you create your first erotica story, and what was it about?

Well, my first story wasn't fully erotica, more a romance story. In fact, I never thought that one day I would write anything steamy. Not at all. I was shy, and grew up in an environment, where everything was taboo. Sharing my views on sex with anyone, let alone write about it? No way...

And yet, I soon had to realize that writing romantic stories couldn't happen without the couple getting it on eventually. Especially because the first four books series I created was about the same characters, and they are 100 pages each (which is a lot to go without including a sex scene every now and again). I must admit, I delayed the inevitable for as long as I could, just to realize later how much I enjoyed writing about sex.

Although my first attempts were very timid indeed, I tried to avoid being too explicit or descriptive. I concentrated on the romantic and paranormal aspect of it (the main characters dream about each other, and somehow when I was writing about the dreams, they gave me courage to be a bit braver).

But it wasn't until I started writing my erotic short stories in 2015, when I started to experiment. Well, if you have a look at 'The Good Neighbour', you can see how my explicitness and mood changed throughout the series.

I think I can say that this was the very first fully erotic story I created, fulfilling one of my secret fantasies (no, I don't have a hot neighbour, or at least I don't think I have, but the idea always fascinated me).

2. What (or who) inspired you to start writing erotica?

My own lack of courage, if I'm honest. All my friends were so open about their relationships and their fantasies, so I thought:

"Why do I have to be this way, when I want to explore everything that's out there?"

And as I have always enjoyed writing, I decided to try it out on paper. It started as a therapy I prescribed for myself, and then it escalated, taking me to places I never thought I would visit. I must say that I'm really glad I gave in to temptation.

3. What do you find most challenging when writing these stories?

To let them go when I finish writing them. I believe that it isn't possible, especially when I create a longer story. The characters, the feelings stay with me long after, as they become part of me for at least a little while.

Another aspect of it is that I keep thinking about what others read into them, and whether they convey their meaning in a way that I intended them to. But, just like when you give birth to a child, when writing a story as well you need to give it space after some time.

I once read a quotation (not sure where, or who said it, but it made me smile and I could definitely relate):

"I met the man of my dreams last night.. in chapter five…" *Sigh*

4. Do you write in other genres, and if yes, then would you consider mixing them with erotica?

Yes, and not sure. I ghost-write for a living, as well as create my own stories, which include romance, horror, thriller, fantasy, crime and more, but I'm not sure it would feel right to mix them with erotica. Mind that, I have had some strange requests that were a mixture, like fetish-horror, but it didn't actually include erotica. I suppose it could have, as it was about a foot fetish, which seems to be quite popular. Oh well, another thing to look at in the future :)

My favourite ones are psychological thrillers though, so I could probably turn one of those into erotica, but at the moment I'm thinking of a transition, rather than a mix. So, for example it would start as a thriller, but have a sexual ending. Hmm…

5. Have you written any stories that were inspired by real life events?

Yes. In fact, my very first story, 'Her First and Last Secret Admirer' (the four books I mentioned earlier) started with an actual recurring medieval dream, which I then implemented into the plot, creating a story and background for it. If it wasn't for that urge to put the whole thing into writing, I probably would never have picked up the courage to write at all. Now it is both in print and on Kindle, so I guess it was a nice bargain :)

I think that writing about real events, twisting them a little, but still keeping them close to your heart is an important process.

Also, that way you can relive those events over and over again, and others will keep guessing what was the real part in it.

Strangely enough, it adds to its mystery (and excitement, of course)...

6. What is your speciality and why?

I would say it's mixing the past with the present. I'm not an expert, but I also love to keep up the suspense until the end. Although this doesn't always come through in my erotic stories, as they are linear, but in my paranormal romance books, I draw a parallel between what happened 500 years ago and what's happening right now. It's difficult to explain without revealing the plot itself, but I do love to play with the mind of the reader, if you know what I mean.

7. Are there any topics you don`t like writing about?

Now? Not really. If you asked me a few years ago, I would have said everything that involves sex ;)

I guess I just realized that I shouldn't say no, just because I don't know how something feels. If I don't try it, I will never know... If I'm not familiar with a topic, then

I do my research, but not too many things scare me nowadays (without wanting to sound weird or vain).

8. Do you have any tips / warnings for newbie erotica writers?

Follow your dreams. You will get some ugly feedback (or none at all), but that doesn't mean that your work isn't appreciated. Don't take them personally, but accept them, so that they can serve as stepping stones, helping you improve your writing. We all make mistakes; that's what makes us human.

Personally, I couldn't wait to grab a physical copy of my books, and that made up for whatever negativity I got (but luckily it has only been minor stuff so far).

So, if you are thinking about writing, or if you already have a story or two, try to make them into a book, no matter how tiny it is. Trust me, as soon as you have it on your shelf, you will become a different person.

9. What is your favourite season and why?

Spring, because that's when everything comes to life. I just love to watch the flowers blossom and the world wake up from its winter slumber. I always feel like I'm reborn myself every time springs comes (I know, I'm a hopeless romantic).

www.ingramcontent.com/pod-product-compliance
Lightning Source LLC
Chambersburg PA
CBHW071251150726

48001CB00018B/1082